Nobody's Friend

Carol Gorman

Illustrated by Rudy Nappi

Publishing House
St. Louis

Published by Concordia Publishing House
3558 S. Jefferson Avenue, St. Louis, MO 63118-3968
Manufactured in the United States of America

Library of Congress Cataloging-in-Publication Data

Gorman, Carol.
    Nobody's friend / Carol Gorman : illustrated by Rudy Nappi.
       (The Tree house kids)
    Summary: When Angie's second grade classmates hear that her father has been arrested, they ostracize her until Mrs. Pilkington reminds the Tree House Kids how to help Jesus by helping their friend.
    ISBN 0-570-04729-3
    [1. Prejudices—Fiction. 2. Friendship—Fiction. 3. Christian life—Fiction.] I. Nappi, Rudy, ill. II. Title. III. Series: Gorman, Carol. Tree house kids.
PZ7.G6693No   1993
[E]—dc20   92-24936

1 2 3 4 5 6 7 8 9 10   02 01 00 99 98 97 96 95 94 93

To good friends
Bob, Michelle, Davis, and Kristine Thomsen

THE TREE HOUSE KIDS

Series

Contents

Terrible News

"Did you hear the news?" Tess said. "It's *horrible!* I just can't *believe* it!"

"What?" said Ben.

Tess, dressed in blue jeans and a long-sleeved pink shirt, was waiting for Ben on the sidewalk in front of her house. Ben lived next door, and they nearly always walked to school together.

Tess looked worried. The strands of hair that didn't get brushed into her ponytail blew wildly around her head in the breeze.

"My mom had the news on this morning," said Tess. "There was a robbery at the 7-Eleven last night!"

"Really?" said Ben.

That really *was* news. Brookdale was a

small, peaceful town, where there was very little crime.

"Yeah," said Tess as they started down the sidewalk. "A man came in the 7-Eleven. He had a gun and told the guy working behind the counter to hand over the money."

"Wow!" said Ben. "I bet he was scared."

"Especially when the robber shot his gun!" said Tess.

Ben's mouth popped open. "Did he get hurt?"

"No," Tess said. "The robber shot the gun into the ceiling."

"Wow!" Ben said again.

"But you haven't heard the really horrible part!" said Tess. She walked sideways so she could look at Ben while she told him the story.

"What?" Ben asked.

"The police caught the robber!" said Tess.

"That's not horrible," Ben said. "I'm glad they caught him!"

"No, be quiet and let me tell you!" said Tess. "You know who the robber was?"

"Who?" Ben asked.

Tess put a hand on Ben's arm and stopped him right in the middle of the sidewalk. "His name is Howard Clymer," said Tess. "That's Angie Clymer's *father!*"

"Angie Clymer?" said Ben. "From our class?"

"Yeah," Tess said.

"How do you know it was Angie's father?" Ben asked.

"Because," Tess said, "the guy on the radio said he was Howard Clymer, of some address on Green Street. Angie lives on Green Street!"

"That *is* where she lives!" said Ben.

"My mom says Angie's father's name is Howard," Tess said. "Mom worked with Angie's mother on the PTA last year."

"I just can't believe it," Ben said. "Angie's so nice!"

"And quiet," said Tess. "I think she's kind of shy."

"How could Angie's father be a robber?" Ben said. "Robbers aren't nice people!"

"I know," Tess said.

There was a long silence. Then Ben and Tess began to walk again.

"I bet Angie's father will go to prison," said Ben after a while. "Angie must really be scared."

10

"I wonder if she's mad at her dad," said Tess.

"She must've been surprised," said Ben. "Who would think her own dad would do something so awful?"

They rounded the corner and found Roger Quinn waiting at the edge of the woods.

Roger looked at his watch. "You're late!" he shouted at them. "Exactly four minutes and"—he gazed off and squinted while he thought—"and 42 seconds later than you were yesterday!"

"Sorry," Ben said.

Ben, Tess, and Roger were the best of friends. Ben and Tess were both in the third grade at Lincoln Elementary, and Roger was in the second grade. Ben and Tess had met Roger on the first day of school this year.

A tough fourth grader, Brad Garth, had beaten up on Roger in the woods along the shortcut to school. He even took his lunch money. Ben, Tess, and Roger had started walking to school together to protect each other. They'd formed a club, The Tree House Kids, to figure out what to do about Brad.

After the problem with Brad Garth had been taken care of, the kids decided to keep on having their club meetings. They liked playing together in the big tree house over Mrs. Pilkington's yard.

Roger looked at his watch again. "Usually you two get here between 8:37 and 8:42," he said. "So I always time myself to get here right at 8:37. That way, I never have to wait more than five minutes. But today I waited *nine* minutes! Almost 10!"

Tess trudged along next to the two boys. "You sure are smart, Roger," she said.

"Thanks," Roger said. He grinned over his big glasses, which had slid down his nose. He tapped the glasses back up with his finger.

"We were late," Ben said, "because we were talking about the robbery at the 7-Eleven."

"Talking shouldn't make you late," Roger pointed out. "You can walk and talk at the same time."

"Did you hear about it?" Tess asked him.

"Yes," Roger said. "It was on the radio this morning."

"Did you recognize the name of the robber?" Ben said.

"No," Roger said. His eyes got big behind his glasses. "Do you *know* him?"

"He's Angie Clymer's father," Tess said. "Angie's in our class."

"*Really?* Yeahhh," Roger said, remembering. "I know who she is! Isn't she kind of short?"

"Yeah," Ben said. "And she's got long, brown hair."

"Yeah," Roger said. "She's nice. Her father robbed the 7-Eleven? I can't believe it!"

"Neither could we," said Tess.

"Do you think the Clymers needed money?" Roger asked. "Is that why her dad robbed the store?"

"Well," Ben said, "they're not rich, but I don't think they're poor."

"Yeah," said Tess. "I think they're kind of in the middle between rich and poor."

"So why would Mr. Clymer rob the 7-Eleven if they don't need the money?" asked Roger. "That isn't logical." He liked everything to make sense.

"I don't know," Ben said. "I don't get it, either."

When Ben, Tess, and Roger arrived at school, all the kids on the playground were talking about Angie Clymer's father and the robbery at the 7-Eleven.

"Do you think she'll come to school today?" Patrick Doyle said.

"She wouldn't *dare* show her face," said Britt Spector, "after what her father did. My mom doesn't want me to play with her anymore."

"Why not?" Tess said.

"My mom says you're known by the company you keep," said Britt.

"Yeah," said Rebecca Holt. "My mom and dad said I have plenty of other friends, and I should play with them instead."

"Mom said to be nice to Angie but not to play with her," added Britt.

"But *Angie* didn't rob the store!" said Ben. "Her father did!"

"Wait a minute," said Kara LaMasters. "We don't know *for sure* that her father robbed the store."

"Yeah," said Roger. "I think he's supposed to be innocent until somebody *proves* he did it."

Rececca Holt rolled her eyes. "Everybody

knows Mr. Clymer robbed the 7-Eleven! The police caught him running out of the store with the money!"

"Of course he's guilty!" said Britt.

"Hey!" a boy yelled halfway across the playground. "Here she comes! Angie's here!"

There was a sudden silence on the playground as Angie stepped out of a dark blue car. She glanced over at all the kids on the playground, who were staring at her. Then she looked down at the ground.

"Is that her mother driving?" Ben whispered to Tess.

"Huh-uh," said Tess. "I don't know who that is. Maybe it's her grandma."

Angie stopped in the middle of the street and turned toward the car. The woman behind the wheel rolled down the window and said something in a voice so quiet no one could hear.

Angie looked very upset. She seemed to be arguing with her.

"I'll be here to pick you up right after school, honey," the woman said in a louder voice, a voice that said that's that. Then she rolled up her window and glided away in her car.

Angie stood alone in the middle of the street and watched the car drive away. She stood there stiffly, not looking to one side or the other, just staring after the blue car.

Then, after a moment or two, she lowered her head, stared at the ground, and began her slow walk toward the school.

Ben had never heard the playground so quiet. The only sound was the scuffing of Angie's sneakers on the sidewalk as she headed toward the brick building.

Angie never looked up once during that long walk. She moved along slowly, watching the ground just in front of her feet.

She passed alongside the crowd of kids watching her. She was so close, Ben could have reached out and touched her. But he didn't.

He thought Angie probably didn't want to talk to anybody. She probably felt very ashamed of what her father had done. She probably felt embarrassed.

Ms. Conley, who taught Ben and Tess's class, came hurrying out to meet Angie and walk with her into the school. Angie hardly looked up at her teacher, but she let Ms. Conley take hold of her hand.

Angie and Ms. Conley disappeared inside Lincoln School.

"I can't believe she came!" said Rebecca.

"I can't either," said Tess. "I wouldn't have come if my mom robbed the 7-Eleven."

"Your mom wouldn't do such a horrible thing," said Rebecca.

"I would just *die* if she did," said Tess.

"Nobody's going to be her friend now," said Nikki Bremer.

"*I'm* sure not," said Rich Adams. "Her dad's a thief!

"You're known by the company you keep," said Britt Spector.

Ben looked over at Tess and Roger. They looked the way he felt.

Very, very sad.

Who's Friends with Angie?

It was a strange day at school. Instead of tromping into the classroom, talking and laughing the way they usually did, the kids walked quietly into the third-grade room. They talked in whispers. Everyone looked around for Angie.

She wasn't there. Ms. Conley, who had been standing in the hall while the kids put their coats away in their lockers, walked into the room and up to the front to her desk.

"Where do you think Angie is?" Ben said in a soft voice to Tess.

"I don't know," Tess said. "Do you think Ms. Conley sent her to the principal's office?"

Ben's eyes got big. "You mean, to get

18

yelled at?" he said. "Her father's the thief, not Angie!"

"I don't mean the principal's yelling at her!" said Tess, rolling her eyes. "Maybe Mr. Evans wanted to say something nice to make Angie feel better."

"Oh," said Ben. "Maybe."

Tess looked up and grabbed Ben's arm. "Here she is," she said.

The whispers in the classroom hushed as Angie moved into the room. Mrs. Dixon, the school counselor, was with her, but she stopped in the doorway and waved cheerfully to Ms. Conley.

"Good morning," Ms. Conley called out to Mrs. Dixon. "Come on in, Angie." Then she turned to the kids, who were standing in silent little groups around the room. "Okay, folks, it's time to get started. Take your seats."

Mrs. Dixon disappeared down the hall. The kids, including Angie, moved to their seats and sat down.

Ms. Conley acted as if nothing had happened. In fact, if Ben hadn't seen Ms. Conley hurry out of the school to meet Angie this morning, he would have thought Ms. Conley didn't even know about the robbery.

Ms. Conley started the school day with reading, as usual. Today was Wednesday, so she worked with the blue group in the back of the room.

Angie was in the yellow group, so she sat at her desk in the middle of the room and stared down at the reading book on her desk. Ben tried to read and work at his seat, but he kept looking over at Angie. She sat stiffly, hardly moving a muscle. She didn't turn over even one page during the whole reading time.

Ben knew Angie wasn't reading. How could she? How could she think about reading when her dad was in jail? And everybody in the whole world knew about it.

Then it was time for science. The kids had been working for several days in groups. Each group was going to give a report on one of the planets.

Ben was in the Mars group. Tess was in the Venus group. Angie was in the Saturn group.

Ben had a hard time concentrating on Mars. He kept peeking over at Angie in her

Saturn group. There were two other kids in her group, Rich Adams and Britt Spector.

Rich and Britt leaned in together, talking. They didn't seem to want Angie to work with them. They didn't look at her or talk to her.

Angie sat back in her chair and stared at the floor. She blinked a lot and sniffed a couple of times. Ben was pretty sure she was crying.

Ms. Conley walked over after a few minutes and spoke softly to Rich, Britt, and Angie. Rich didn't say anything, but Britt rolled her eyes and turned to Angie. Angie scooted her chair closer but still stared at the floor.

For the rest of science class, most of the kids in the room were watching the Saturn group. Nobody was getting much work done.

Britt asked Angie what she wanted to tell about Saturn in the report. Angie shrugged, still staring at the floor. Then Rich asked her what notes she had about Saturn. Angie slowly opened her folder and looked through it. Then she closed it and said something very softly.

"You left them at *home!*" Britt wailed

loudly. "How can you work with us if you don't have your notes!"

Angie's face crumpled, and she let out a sob. She jumped up from her chair, ran out of the room, and disappeared down the hall.

All the kids turned to their teacher. Ms. Conley looked almost as upset as Angie. She took a deep breath and stood up at her desk.

"Ben, will you be the class monitor for a few minutes?" she said. Ben nodded. "Everyone, please get back to work. I'll be right back." She hurried out of the room and turned down the hall in the direction Angie had run.

Of course, the kids didn't get back to work. They talked instead. They talked about Angie.

"Where do you think Angie went?" Tess said.

"I bet she ran home," said Nikki.

"Do you think she'll get in trouble with the principal?" said Patrick.

"No, but *Britt* probably will," said Tess, glaring at Britt, who sat across the room with Rich.

"What do you mean?" Britt demanded.

"You yelled at her for not having her notes," said Tess.

"How can she work with us if she leaves her stuff at home!" cried Britt.

"Her stuff!" Tess said. "The last thing Angie's thinking about is her stuff! Her father's in *jail*, for pete's sake!"

"That's not *my* problem," said Britt.

"Yeah," said Adam. "We want to get a good grade on our report."

"Why are you sticking up for Angie anyway?" Britt said to Tess. "If you stick up for her, you're just like her!"

"What's *that* supposed to mean?" Tess yelled.

"Her father's a robber!" said Britt. "A jailbird! I'm not even supposed to play with her!"

"Birds of a feather flock together," said Rich.

"You're known by the company you keep," said Britt. "Are *you* a robber too, Tess?"

"What!" Tess cried.

"Somebody took my favorite blue pen off my desk last week," said Britt. "Maybe Angie took it. Or maybe *you* took it!"

"I did *not!*" yelled Tess.

"Well, you seem to like her so much," Britt started to say.

"Hey, you guys," said Ben. "Come on, be quiet. We're supposed to be working."

But the kids paid no attention to him.

Tess stood up at her desk. "I can like anybody I want to like!" she hollered.

"Well, nobody will be your friend if you hang around with Angie," said Britt.

"That's stupid!" said Tess.

"If you're friends with Angie," said Britt, "nobody will want to play with you. We're not supposed to play with Angie, so we won't play with you either."

"I don't care!" yelled Tess.

"Okay," said Britt. She turned to the rest of the kids. "Tess doesn't care if she's friends with you guys anymore!"

But Ben saw the look on Tess's face and knew that Tess *did* care. Tess cared very much. She wanted to have friends, just like everybody else.

Britt was a popular girl, and she was a leader in the third-grade class. The kids, especially the girls, followed her. If Britt

25

wanted to do something, the rest of the kids usually wanted to do it too.

If Britt stopped being Tess's friend, a lot of the other kids wouldn't play with Tess either.

Ben's stomach felt bad all of a sudden. He didn't blame Angie for what her father did. But still, it was going to be hard to have Angie in the class from now on. If he and Tess stayed friends with Angie, would they lose the rest of their friends?

Ben slid down in his seat and put his head in his hands. What were he and Tess going to do?

3

Forgiveness and Peanut Butter Cookies

"We'd better have a meeting of The Tree House Kids," said Ben on the way home. "This is a problem as bad as when Brad was beating up everybody."

"Yeah," said Tess. "Maybe if we all think really hard, we can figure out what to do about Angie. I like her, and I feel sorry for her."

"Yeah," said Roger, "but you don't want to lose all your other friends."

The kids crossed Roger's yard and tromped into Mrs. Pilkington's yard. One by one, they climbed the fence next to her garage, pulled themselves onto the roof, then stepped over into the tree house.

"Hey!" cried Ben. "What's this?"

The three kids bent over the large paper bag sitting in the middle of the tree-house floor. The top of the bag had been folded over once very neatly.

"What's inside?" said Tess.

"Open it," said Roger.

Ben unfolded the top of the sack and peeked in. Then he reached in and brought out a bundle wrapped in foil.

He grinned. "It's warm," he said.

He unwrapped the foil. "Cookies!" he said. He sniffed them. "Peanut butter!"

"Great!" said Tess. "I'm starved. Pass the cookies, please."

"And there's a thermos here too," Ben said. He reached back in the bag. "Here's a note! It's taped to the thermos."

"What does it say?" asked Roger.

"Pass the cookies, Ben," Tess said again.

Ben passed the cookies to Tess and held up the note.

" 'Here's a treat for some of my favorite friends, The Tree House Kids,' " read Ben. "It's signed 'Mrs. P.' "

"What a *nice* lady!" Tess said, her mouth packed full of cookies.

"Let's invite her to come up," said Ben.

"Hey, yeah," said Roger. "Maybe she'll know what to do about Angie Clymer."

"Good idea," said Tess, standing up. "I'll go get her. Don't eat all the cookies while I'm gone."

"We'll save you one," said Ben. He nudged Roger and grinned. "Right, Roger?"

"Right!" Roger said.

"One!" cried Tess. "Hey, there are at least a dozen cookies there!"

"Just kidding," said Ben, grinning. "Go get Mrs. P."

"Be right back," Tess said. She stepped carefully onto the garage roof and disappeared over the side.

"If anyone'll know what to do about Angie," Ben said, "it'll be Mrs. P."

"Right," Roger said.

In a few minutes Tess returned, and soon Mrs. Pilkington's gray-haired head popped over the side of the tree-house wall.

"Thanks for the cookies and cocoa, Mrs. P.!" said Ben.

"That was a great surprise!" Roger said.

"You're most welcome," Mrs. Pilkington said, seating herself cross-legged on the

floor with the kids. "I thought you three just might stop by for a meeting today. Did you sing your new theme song?"

"No," said Tess seriously. "We're not exactly in the mood for singing. We have a problem."

"Oh?" said Mrs. P.

"Yeah," Roger said. "A *big* problem."

Tess, Ben, and Roger told Mrs. Pilkington about the robbery at the 7-Eleven. Mrs. P. had heard about it on the news.

Then they told her that the man who was caught was Angie Clymer's father.

"Oh, dear," said Mrs. Pilkington. "The poor girl."

"Yeah," said Ben. "We feel sorry for her. But the other kids won't play with her."

"Britt and Rebecca said their mothers told them not to," said Tess.

"Oh, that's very sad," said Mrs. P.

"Yeah," said Ben. "Britt keeps saying, 'You're known by the company you keep.' "

"Do you think we should stay away from Angie too?" Tess asked.

"Oh, my, no!" said Mrs. Pilkington. "Angie needs friends now more than ever."

"I just don't get it," said Ben. "Why would Angie's father rob the 7-Eleven?"

"I don't know," said Mrs. P. "There could be many reasons. He must be having money problems."

"But having a reason doesn't make it right!" said Tess.

"No, it doesn't," said Mrs. Pilkington.

"But only *bad* people steal," said Ben. "I can't believe Angie's father is bad. Angie's so nice!"

Mrs. P. thought a moment before she spoke. "Well, Angie's father did a bad thing, but we all do bad things at times. That's the way we are."

"Huh?" said Tess. "I don't get it."

"Sometimes people make bad mistakes," said Mrs. Pilkington. "They need our forgiveness. God forgives them, you know."

"Yeah," said Tess. "But sometimes forgiving people is really hard! Take my dumb sister. She's always bugging me, and she hogs all the space in our room. She drives me *crazy!*"

Mrs. P. smiled. "Sure," she said. "We can have arguments with our parents and brothers and sisters and friends. But we still love them and forgive them, don't we?"

"Well, I guess so," said Tess, rolling her eyes. "But I would sure never tell that to Ashley."

Mrs. Pilkington leaned forward and smiled. "You know what? God loves Angie's father very much! In fact, He loves Mr. Clymer just as much as He loves you and me."

"God loves a *robber* as much as me?" said Tess, her eyes opened wide.

"That's right," said Mrs. P. "He loves us all the same."

"Even the meanest person in the world?" asked Roger.

"Even a murderer?" asked Tess.

"Even a murderer," said Mrs. Pilkington. "I'm sure God is very unhappy about the horrible things a murderer does. But He loves that person just the same as He loves your pastor, or your teacher, or *you.*"

"Wow!" said Ben. "I always thought God loved pastors the most."

"He loves us all the same," said Mrs. Pilkington. "And He wants the very best for us.

God's Holy Spirit gives us His love and helps us to love one another."

"Boy," said Tess. She shook her head.

"What, Tess?" said Mrs. Pilkington.

"My Mom says that God is love," Tess said. "I guess God really *is* love, if He loves all the *bad* guys in the world as much as the *good* guys."

Mrs. Pilkington smiled. "That's what God's all about, Tess," she said. "That's why He sent His only Son to save us all. Every one of us."

"But what should we do about the other kids, Mrs. P.?" asked Tess. "What if we stay friends with Angie and they won't play with us?"

"I don't think they'll turn away from you," said Mrs. Pilkington. "Haven't you been friends with those kids for a long time?"

"Since kindergarten!" said Tess.

Mrs. Pilkington nodded. "There might be a few kids at first who say nasty things or don't want to play," she said.

Tess rolled her eyes. "That'll be Britt and Rebecca," she said.

"And Rich," said Ben.

"But if you three are good to Angie and nice to everyone else," said Mrs. P., "including Britt and Rebecca and—who's the other kid?"

"Rich," said Ben.

"Oh yes," said Mrs. P. "Well, I don't think you'll lose any friends."

"We have to be nice to Britt?" said Tess.

"Yup," said Mrs. P.

"Boy, that won't be easy," said Tess.

Mrs. P. laughed. "You can do it, Tess," she said. "You won't need to say anything to the other kids, but you can *show* them how to act with Angie. I think they'll follow you."

"You really think it'll work?" said Roger.

Mrs. Pilkington smiled. "Yes, I do," she said. "And won't Angie feel good to have such loyal friends!"

"Yeah," Tess said, smiling.

"Yeah," said Roger.

"I feel a lot better, Mrs. P.," said Ben. He looked at her. "You always seem to know what to do about stuff. Problem stuff with people."

Mrs. Pilkington smiled. "Ben, the best way to figure out what to do when you have a problem with people is to ask yourself, 'What's the *loving* thing to do?' If you think about how God loves you and how you like to be treated, you'll always do the right thing."

"Yeah," Ben said. "I guess you're right. Thanks."

"My pleasure," said Mrs. Pilkington.

Roger looked at Mrs. P., then at Ben and Tess. "Well," he said, "that's another good meeting of The Tree House Kids."

Tess grinned. "Even though we didn't sing the theme song."

"I'm more in the mood to sing now," said Ben.

"Me too," said Roger.

"I'll sing too," said Mrs. P.

"So what are we waiting for?" said Tess.

So all together, to the tune of "America, the Beautiful," they sang:

The Tree House Kids, The Tree House Kids,
To you we are true blue!
We get along, we sing this song,
Up here there's such a view!

Whenever times are hard or bad,
Our helping hands we lend.

Here is a clue, we stick like glue,
We always have a friend!

Playing with Angie

"What do you think'll happen?" said Tess on the way to school the next day.

"You mean with Angie?" Ben said.

"Yeah," Tess said. "And the other kids. If we're really nice to Angie, I wonder how the other kids will act."

"Yeah," said Roger. "I was thinking about that too."

"I'm kind of nervous," said Ben.

"Me too," said Roger.

"Let's just go right up to Angie," said Tess, "and ask her to play a game of four-square or something."

"Okay," said Ben.

"If the other kids won't play with us after that, we still have each other," said Tess.

"Right," said Roger.

"Right," said Ben.

"And we'll still have Angie for a friend," said Ben.

"Right," said Roger and Tess.

The kids shuffled along the sidewalk in silence for a few minutes. They were trying to keep their spirits up, but deep inside, all three kids were worried. They were worried that Britt and Rebecca and Rich might tell others not to play with them.

Then they'd be alone, just the four of them.

When they got to school, the playground was filled with kids. They were playing tetherball, hopscotch, and basketball. They were playing on the swings and the slide and the jungle gym. They gathered in pairs and in groups, and the air was filled with the sounds of bouncing balls, chatter, and laughter.

Tess looked over the playground, her eyes squinting in the bright sunlight.

"Where's Angie?" she said.

"I don't see her," said Roger.

"Maybe she isn't here yet," said Ben.

Tess looked at her watch. "It's almost time for the bell. She should be here by now."

"Maybe she went inside with Ms. Conley again," Ben said.

"Yeah, maybe we'll see her inside," Tess said.

Just the same, the kids watched for Angie on the playground during the last few minutes before the bell. They even looked for her among the clumps of bushes at the edge of the playground. They thought she might feel like hiding from everybody. Among the bushes was a good place to be alone.

But she wasn't there either.

When the bell rang, the kids trooped inside with everyone else. Angie wasn't at her locker.

Ben and Tess said good-bye to Roger, and he went to the second-grade room. They walked into their third-grade room.

Angie wasn't in the classroom.

"Maybe she'll come in with Mrs. Dixon again," said Ben.

But when Ms. Conley started the school day with reading, Angie still wasn't there. And she didn't come in with the counselor. Tess looked at Ben across the room, and he shrugged.

It looked as if Angie wasn't coming to

school today. Maybe it was so bad for her yesterday, she just couldn't come today.

Ben didn't blame her. He wouldn't have wanted to come to school, either, if his father had robbed the 7-Eleven. And he *really* wouldn't have wanted to come to school if the kids were mean to him. Britt had been really mean to Angie yesterday.

Poor Angie. Her father was in jail, and her friends weren't playing with her. How miserable could anyone get?

"I think we should go over to Angie's house," said Ben after school. "Let's show her we like her and ask her to play with us."

Ben, Tess, and Roger had met out on the sidewalk after school. Angie hadn't shown up all day.

"That's a good idea," Tess said. "She must be afraid to come to school. She's afraid that Britt and those guys will be mean to her."

"Then she's right," Ben said. "I heard Britt say she was glad Angie didn't have the nerve to come to school today."

"Britt is such a jerk!" cried Tess. She

looked at Ben. "Do you really think that God loves *her* as much as He loves Angie?"

"I guess so," Ben said, shrugging. "It's pretty hard to believe though."

"Yeah," said Roger. "It sure is."

"Let's go to Angie's house and ask her to play," said Tess. She thought a moment. "Britt won't see us playing with her there."

"Yeah," said Ben, "but when Angie comes back to school, Britt—and everybody—will see us playing with her."

"Yeah," said Tess, gloomily. "I know." She sighed. "I sure hope everybody isn't mean to us too."

"Yeah," said Ben.

"Let's ask her to go to the park," said Roger.

"Yeah," said Tess. "If someone's going to see us with her and be mean, I guess we should get it over with."

"Okay," said Ben.

The three kids trooped along the sidewalk. In 15 minutes, they stood in front of Angie's house. It was a small, white house with a little flower garden at the side.

"You don't think her father's here, do you?" Tess said nervously.

time the kids had seen her smile at all since her father robbed the 7-Eleven.

"Okay," she said softly.

"Good," said her mother. Ben thought her mother looked even happier than Angie did. "Be sure to take your jacket, honey. It's getting chilly."

Angie got her jacket, and the kids headed to the park.

"I like the monkeys best," said Tess.

"That's because they look like you," teased Ben.

"Yeah, right!" cried Tess. She glanced over at Angie. Angie didn't seem to have heard Ben's joke. She walked along, thinking her own thoughts.

The four kids arrived at the park and headed for the zoo. The monkey house was in the middle of the zoo. First, the kids visited the goats, then the zebra, and then the ducks at the edge of the pond.

"Now the monkeys!" said Tess. The kids tromped up the sidewalk and entered the monkey house.

Tess drew in a sharp breath and grabbed Ben's and Roger's arms. They looked up to

see Rebecca Holt and Tam Ling standing at the far end of the monkey house.

Rebecca looked up and saw them with Angie Clymer, and her mouth dropped open. She nudged Tam's arm and nodded at the four kids.

Tess didn't think Angie saw Rebecca and Tam. She turned Angie away and pointed to a small monkey in the corner of the huge cage.

"See the little one over there?" she said. "He's my favorite. I call him Ed. I wish I could take him home with me."

Ben hoped Rebecca wouldn't say anything mean. He kept the conversation going. "Tess, your mom wouldn't want any more monkeys in the house," he said. "One is enough!"

"I'd rather share my room with old Ed than my stupid sister," said Tess.

"*I can't believe it!*" Rebecca whispered from across the monkey house. Her voice was loud enough that the kids could hear every word. "It's Angie Clymer!"

Angie turned toward Rebecca when she heard her name. "Come on, Angie," Tess said, putting an arm around her shoulder.

"It's getting stuffy in here. Let's go back outside."

Ben and Roger followed the girls out of the monkey house.

Tess continued to walk with Angie, her arm still around the girl's shoulder. Angie looked straight ahead, her eyes filled with hurt.

"I want to go home now," Angie said. The corners of her mouth turned down as if she was about to cry.

"Okay," Tess said. She gave Angie's shoulder a gentle squeeze. "Angie, we're your friends, okay?"

Angie nodded and looked for half a second over at Tess. "Yeah," she said softly.

Ben and Roger hurried to catch up with the girls.

"I can't believe it!" they heard Rebecca say loudly. The kids didn't look back, but they knew that she and Tam had followed them outside the monkey house.

"Angie Clymer's at the zoo!" Rebecca was yelling now. "Along with her *very good friends*, Ben and Tess! *Wait till the kids hear about this!*"

Tess, Ben, and Roger walked with Angie.

No one said anything all the way to Angie's house.

At Angie's front door, Tess stopped her.

"Angie, we'll stop by and walk to school with you tomorrow," said Tess.

Angie's eyelashes fluttered while she blinked back tears. She made a gulping noise in her throat.

"How about 8:51?" said Roger. "We could be here by then." He glanced over at Ben and Tess. "That is, if these two guys aren't late."

"Okay, Angie?" Ben said. "We'll be here to pick you up."

Tess looked up to see Angie's mother in the window. She must have been watching for them.

"Okay, Angie?" Tess said.

Angie nodded. "Okay," she said in a whisper.

Then she opened the front door and, without another word, disappeared inside.

Showing the Way

It was a long walk to school the next morning.

Ben, Tess, and Roger stopped to meet Angie at her house, and the four of them trudged along in silence.

Ben, Tess, and Roger were wondering what mean things Rebecca and Britt might say when they got to the playground. And they were very worried that the rest of the kids wouldn't play with them.

Each of them sneaked looks at Angie while they walked along. She looked very sad and scared. The closer they got to the school, the more she stared down at the sidewalk. Ben decided that Angie didn't want to see anyone. And she probably wished no one would see her either.

When they were two blocks from school, Ben decided he should say something. Maybe he could cheer Angie up a little before they got to school.

"Knock, knock," Ben said.

Nobody answered. A half-minute went by. The only sound was four pairs of sneakers scuffing the sidewalk.

"I have a joke," Ben said finally. "Knock, knock."

Roger shook his head. Tess sighed loudly. Angie continued to stare at the ground.

No one felt like hearing jokes.

"Come on, you guys," Ben said. "Knock, knock."

Tess rolled her eyes. "Somebody'd better play along," she said, "or he'll *never* give up."

"Who's there?" Roger said.

"You," said Ben.

"You who?" said Roger.

"Oh, are you calling me?" said Ben.

Ben was the only one who laughed.

"I heard that from my dad," Ben started to say. Then he thought about Angie and *her* father and wished he'd stayed quiet.

Angie bit her lip and walked with her head down.

Tess and Roger shook their heads at Ben. The joke was a bad idea.

The four kids walked along in silence the rest of the way to school.

The playground was crowded when they arrived. Britt and Rebecca were leaning against the flagpole, talking. When they saw Angie they stopped talking and stared.

"She came back," said Britt, loud enough for Angie to hear. "I never thought Angie would show her face around here again."

"I didn't either," said Rebecca. "And look who she's *with*."

"Doesn't surprise me," said Britt. "Birds of a feather flock together."

Ben looked over at the girls. "Angie's one of us," he said.

Britt's mouth dropped open and Rebecca gasped.

Ben kept his head held high and led his friends past Britt and Rebecca.

Some of the kids on the playground saw Angie and pointed her out to the others. Pretty soon everybody at Lincoln School knew that Angie was back.

And they knew she was with Ben, Tess, and Roger.

For the second time in three days, the playground grew unusually quiet. Most of the kids stopped where they were and stared at Angie, the daughter of a thief.

"Come on," Ben said, putting a hand on Angie's shoulder as they walked. "Let's play four-square."

Angie didn't say anything, and she started blinking back tears. Two tears escaped and trickled down her cheeks.

Staring at the ground, she let Ben guide her down the slope of the playground to the four-square pattern painted on the cement.

Four of Britt's friends were playing four-square, but when Ben, Tess, Roger, and Angie got in line to play, the girls stopped playing and walked away.

It was starting now, Ben thought. The kids weren't going to play with any of them. Maybe never again.

"We'll play," Ben said to Angie. "The four of us."

The kids took their positions in the four squares. Ben served the ball and tapped it gently to Angie. She batted it back to him.

He passed it over to Tess, who shoved it over into Roger's square.

Ben knew that the kids on the playground were watching them. He wondered what would happen the first time in their game someone was "out." There was no one in line to step in and play. He wished *someone* on the playground would join their game.

"Okay," Roger said, after they'd played for a few minutes. "No more Mr. Nice Guy. I'm playing to win now."

He batted the ball hard into the far corner of Ben's square. Ben missed it. He was out.

"Way to go, Roger," Tess said. She forced a smile and tried to look as if she were having a good time.

Tess moved into the server's square, Angie moved up one, and so did Roger.

But there was no one to step into the game. Nobody on the playground moved. The playground was filled with living statues.

Ben moved to the fourth square.

"Hold it, Ben Brophy!" said a voice off to the side.

Ben turned to see Kara LaMasters. She

was a friend of theirs who had been very ill not long ago. She was much better now.

Kara was pretending to be mad. She put her hands on her hips and tried to scowl.

"What's the matter?" said Ben.

"You're out, that's what's the matter," Kara said. "*I'm* in the game now!"

Ben could've cried, he felt so relieved. Kara was going to join the game! Not *all* of the kids were going to be mean like Britt and Rebecca.

Ben grinned at her and stepped out of the fourth square. He looked over at Angie. She looked up at Kara and gave her a tiny smile. Kara grinned back.

The game started again.

Out of the crowd of kids on the playground came Sam Flagg. He quietly stepped into line behind Ben. He grinned over at Angie. She smiled shyly back at him.

Then came Patrick Doyle. He got into line behind Sam.

Then came Alison Whiting and Nikki Bremer. And Tam Ling and Rob McGregor. And Lyle Washington and Tim Roberts and Mandy Tomkins and Cindy Cleaver and Jennifer Wilson.

Before long, Ben's four-square game had the longest line he'd ever seen! Most of the third-grade kids had joined the line and were rooting for their friends.

And the friend who was cheered the most was Angie Clymer.

"Come on, Angie! Get Tess out!"

"Shove that ball hard, Ang!"

"Way to go, Angie!"

Ben had never seen Angie so happy. Her smile got bigger and bigger, and joy shone from her whole self.

Roger grinned at Ben. Tess gave him the thumbs-up sign.

It was working! Mrs. Pilkington was right. The rest of the kids had followed them. They liked Angie and hadn't listened to Britt and Rebecca. They wanted to play! Britt and Rebecca stood back by the tetherball and watched. Only Rich Adams stood with them.

Rich looked over at the long line behind the four-square game, then turned to look at Britt and Rebecca. He gazed back at the long line, and his face changed.

Without saying anything to the girls, he

started walking toward the four-square game.

"Rich!" yelled Britt. "Where do you think you're going?"

Rich didn't answer. He just kept walking.

He didn't stop until he reached the end of the four-square line. Some kids turned around to look at him curiously.

Rich shrugged. "I want to play," he said.

The game continued until it was time for school to start. The line was so long, most of the kids didn't get a chance to play. But that didn't matter.

The game itself hadn't been important.

What was important was letting Angie know she wasn't alone. She had friends, lots of them, who would stand by her.

When the bell rang, the kids surrounded Angie and moved with her across the playground and into the school building.

Angie turned in almost a full circle and looked at all of her friends. She looked so happy that Ben just *knew* she would be all right now. Whatever happened with her father, she'd get through it.

She had friends who cared about her. And she knew it now.

Mrs. Pilkington had been right again, Ben thought. The other kids had followed them. He and Tess and Roger had been good to Angie, and the other kids were too.

Ben thought about how God loves all His children the same. Wouldn't it be great if people everywhere followed God's lead and loved everyone else?

That would really be something.

Ben watched the crowd of kids move off toward the school. Tess and Roger walked over with big grins on their faces. The three headed toward the school building.

Tess, walking between Ben and Roger, put her arms over the shoulders of the two guys.

"This was so great," she said.

"It sure was," said Roger. "Did you see the look on Angie's face when all the kids came over to get in line?"

"Yeah," said Ben. "I wish I had a picture of it."

"I've got a picture of it," Tess said. She pointed to her forehead. "It's in here, in my mind. It's gonna stay there for a long time."

"Yeah, me too," said Roger.

"Well," Ben said. "It'll be good to get back to normal."

"It'll take a while for Angie to get back to normal," Tess said.

"Yeah," Roger said. "Maybe a long, long time. But she'll know she's got us."

"That's right," said Ben. "She's got us."

And we've got her, Ben thought.

Ben and Roger each threw an arm over Tess's shoulder, and The Tree House Kids headed into the school building.